™

& THE HAUNTED HOUSE

SCOOBY-DOO & THE HAUNTED HOUSE

ISBN 1 84023 832 1

Published by Titan Books, a division of
Titan Publishing Group Ltd.
144 Southwark St
London SE1 0UP

SCRIPT: Dan Abnett, Joe Edkih, Brett Lewis,
Robbie Busch, John Rozum, Scott Cunningham
PENCILS: Joe Staton, Don Perlin, Anthony Williams, John Delaney
INKS: Dave Hunt, Dan Davis, Jeff Albrecht, Scott McCrae,
Horacio Ottolini, Andrew Pepoy
LETTERS: John Constanza, Jenna Garcia, Gustav, Gus Hartman,
Sergio Garcia, Tom Orzechowski
COLOURS: Harvey Richards, Paul Becton & Digital Chameleon

A CIP catalogue record for this title is available from
the British Library.

First edition: March 2004

10 9 8 7 6 5 4 3 2 1

Printed in Italy.

What did you think of this book? We love to hear from
our readers. Please email us at: readerfeedback@titanemail.com,
or write to us at the above address. You can also visit us at
www.titanbooks.com

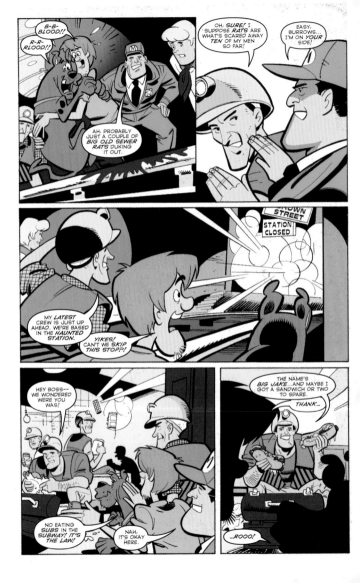

THE TRACKS OF MY FEARS

SCOTT CUNNINGHAM-Writer   JOE STATON-Penciller
ANDREW PEPOY-Inker   JENNA GARCIA-Letterer
PAUL BECTON-Colorist   DIGITAL CHAMELEON-Separations
HARVEY RICHARDS-Asst. Editor   JOAN HILTY-Editor

DCSD163

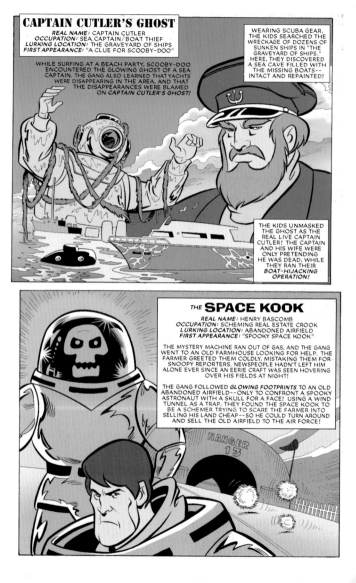

CAPTAIN CUTLER'S GHOST

REAL NAME: CAPTAIN CUTLER
OCCUPATION: SEA CAPTAIN / BOAT THIEF
LURKING LOCATION: THE GRAVEYARD OF SHIPS
FIRST APPEARANCE: "A CLUE FOR SCOOBY-DOO"

WHILE SURFING AT A BEACH PARTY, SCOOBY-DOO ENCOUNTERED THE GLOWING GHOST OF A SEA CAPTAIN. THE GANG ALSO LEARNED THAT YACHTS WERE DISAPPEARING IN THE AREA, AND THAT THE DISAPPEARANCES WERE BLAMED ON *CAPTAIN CUTLER'S GHOST!*

WEARING SCUBA GEAR, THE KIDS SEARCHED THE WRECKAGE OF DOZENS OF SUNKEN SHIPS IN "THE GRAVEYARD OF SHIPS." HERE, THEY DISCOVERED A SEA CAVE FILLED WITH THE MISSING BOATS-- INTACT AND REPAINTED!

THE KIDS UNMASKED THE GHOST AS THE REAL LIVE CAPTAIN CUTLER! THE CAPTAIN AND HIS WIFE WERE ONLY PRETENDING HE WAS DEAD, WHILE THEY RAN THEIR *BOAT-HIJACKING OPERATION!*

THE SPACE KOOK

REAL NAME: HENRY BASCOMB
OCCUPATION: SCHEMING REAL ESTATE CROOK
LURKING LOCATION: ABANDONED AIRFIELD
FIRST APPEARANCE: "SPOOKY SPACE KOOK"

THE MYSTERY MACHINE RAN OUT OF GAS, AND THE GANG WENT TO AN OLD FARMHOUSE LOOKING FOR HELP. THE FARMER GREETED THEM COLDLY, MISTAKING THEM FOR SNOOPY REPORTERS. NEWSPEOPLE HADN'T LEFT HIM ALONE EVER SINCE AN EERIE CRAFT WAS SEEN HOVERING OVER HIS FIELDS AT NIGHT!

THE GANG FOLLOWED *GLOWING* FOOTPRINTS TO AN OLD ABANDONED AIRFIELD--ONLY TO CONFRONT A SPOOKY ASTRONAUT WITH A SKULL FOR A FACE! USING A WIND TUNNEL AS A TRAP, THEY FOUND THE SPACE KOOK TO BE A SCHEMER TRYING TO SCARE THE FARMER INTO SELLING HIS LAND CHEAP--SO HE COULD TURN AROUND AND SELL THE OLD AIRFIELD TO THE AIR FORCE!

HANGER 13

THE TELESCOPE GHOST

REAL NAME: "BLUESTONE THE GREAT"
OCCUPATION: STAGE MAGICIAN/
TREASURE HUNTER
LURKING LOCATION:
VASQUEZ CASTLE ON HAUNTED ISLE
FIRST APPEARANCE: "HASSLE IN
THE CASTLE"

THE GANG ENCOUNTERED A *TALKING SKULL*, A *HAM SANDWICH* APPEARING OUT OF THIN AIR, A *FLYING CARPET*--AND EVENTUALLY DISCOVERED THAT MAGIC TRICKS WERE RESPONSIBLE FOR ALL OF THEM, EXCEPT FOR THE GHOST WHO FLOATED THROUGH WALLS. WHEN THE GHOST WAS REVEALED TO BE THE EX-MAGICIAN "BLUESTONE THE GREAT," HE REVEALED HE DID IT WITH *MIRRORS!*

ON A BOATING TRIP, SCOOBY AND THE GANG RAN AGROUND IN THE FOG AND FOUND THEMSELVES ON SPOOKY HAUNTED ISLE, HOME OF *VASQUEZ CASTLE.* THE 17th-CENTURY PIRATE VASQUEZ ALLEGEDLY HID A TREASURE SOMEWHERE IN THE CASTLE!

THE MAN FROM MARS

REAL NAME: CHARLIE THE FUNLAND ROBOT
OCCUPATION: AMUSEMENT PARK OPERATOR
LURKING LOCATION: FUNLAND AMUSEMENT PARK
FIRST APPEARANCE: "FOUL PLAY IN FUNLAND"

WHILE CLAM-DIGGING NEXT TO A DESERTED AMUSEMENT PARK, SCOOBY AND THE GANG NOTICED RIDES OPERATING WITH NO PASSENGERS. WHEN THEY QUESTIONED THE PARK'S CARETAKER, HE DENIED ANY STRANGE HAPPENINGS. THE GANG THEN SPOTTED A FREAKY-LOOKING CREATURE ATOP THE FERRIS WHEEL THAT WAS SETTING RIDES INTO MOTION!

AFTER CHASING IT AROUND THE FAIRWAY, THE ROLLER COASTER AND THE TUNNEL OF LOVE, THEY DISCOVERED IT WAS A *ROBOT!* THE CARETAKER CONFESSED TO CREATING IT TO RUN THE PARK--AND THE CARETAKER'S *WIFE* CONFESSED TO RIGGING IT TO RUN HAYWIRE, BECAUSE SHE DIDN'T WANT IT AROUND CHILDREN!

THE **WEREWOLF**

REAL NAME: SILAS LONG
OCCUPATION: SHEEP RUSTLER
LURKING LOCATION: CREEPY CAMPSITE
FIRST APPEARANCE: "WHO'S AFRAID OF THE BIG BAD WEREWOLF?"

WHEN THE MYSTERY INC. GANG WENT CAMPING, STRANGE GROWLING SOUNDS LED THEM TO A TRAIL OF *WOLF FOOTPRINTS*--FOOTPRINTS THAT BELONGED TO A WOLF WHO WALKS ON *TWO LEGS!* THEY LED IN TURN TO THE OPENED GRAVE OF *SILAS LONG*--A MAN WHO WAS HALF-MAN AND HALF-WOLF, AND WHO NOW APPARENTLY WALKS AGAIN!

BRAVING BOOBY-TRAPPED BOATHOUSES, BARRELS FITTED WITH BREATHING TUBES, AND OTHER MYSTERIOUS PROPS, THE GANG UNCOVERED A SHEEP RUSTLER'S PLOT OF STEALING SHEEP AND FLOATING THEM DOWNSTREAM IN THE RIGGED BARRELS, TO BE RETRIEVED BY AN ACCOMPLICE!

HERE LIES
...AS LONG
HALF - MAN
AND
HALF - WOLF

THE GIGGLING GREEN **GHOST**

REAL NAME: COSGOOD CREEPS
OCCUPATION: LAWYER
LURKING LOCATION: HAUNTED MANSION
FIRST APPEARANCE: "A NIGHT OF FRIGHT IS NO DELIGHT"

AN ECCENTRIC MILLIONAIRE COLONEL LEFT *ONE MILLION DOLLARS* TO FOUR RELATIVES AND-- SCOOBY-DOO, WHO ONCE RESCUED HIM FROM A FISH POND!

COSGOOD CREEPS, THE ATTORNEY OF THE LATE COLONEL, THEN REVEALED THAT SCOOBY-DOO HAD TO SPEND THE *WHOLE NIGHT* IN THE HAUNTED MANSION TO GET THE MONEY! THE GANG STUCK AROUND AND WOUND UP DEALING WITH *GROWLING FISH, TRAP DOORS, SPOOKY WRITTEN CLUES,* AND A PAIR OF *GIGGLING GREEN GHOSTS!*

TRACES OF GREEN PAINT FROM THE "GHOSTS" LED THE GANG TO SET AN ELABORATE TRAP, REVEALING THE GHOSTS TO BE MR. CREEPS AND HIS PARTNER MR. CRAWLS, WHO PLANNED TO SCARE EVERYONE OFF THE ISLAND AND GRAB THE FORTUNE. UNFORTUNATELY, THAT FORTUNE TURNED OUT TO BE *WORTHLESS CIVIL WAR MONEY!*

THE INDIAN WITCH DOCTOR

REAL NAME: BUCK MASTERS
OCCUPATION: DOG TRAINER
LURKING LOCATION: INDIAN GAP
FIRST APPEARANCE: "DECOY FOR A DOGNAPPER"

THE MYSTERY, INC. GANG WAS CALLED TO A CASE INVOLVING *KIDNAPPED SHOW DOGS.* THE GANG DRESSED SCOOBY-DOO AS A CHAMPION GREAT DANE, IN HOPES THAT SCOOBY-DOO WOULD BE ABDUCTED. THE PLAN SUCCEEDED, AND A *TRACKING DEVICE* IN SCOOBY'S COLLAR LED THE GANG TO A DESERTED PUEBLO INDIAN VILLAGE. THERE, THEY FACED THE MYSTERIOUS *INDIAN WITCH DOCTOR*--WHO TURNED OUT TO BE BUCK MASTERS, A CHAMPION DOG BREEDER! MASTERS PLANNED TO WIN THE DOG SHOW BY KIDNAPPING THE COMPETITION!

THE HAWAIIAN WITCH DOCTOR

REAL NAME: JOHN SIMMS
OCCUPATION: PEARL THIEF
LURKING LOCATION: ANCIENT HAWAIIAN VILLAGE
FIRST APPEARANCE: "A TIKI SCARE IS NO FAIR"

WHILE VACATIONING IN HAWAII, SCOOBY-DOO AND SHAGGY WERE WARNED BY THEIR HOST TO STAY AWAY FROM AN ANCIENT HAUNTED VILLAGE. SOON *GHOST DRUMS* BEGAN TO BEAT, AND A MYSTERIOUS WITCH DOCTOR APPEARED, WARNING EVERYONE THAT THE GOD *MANO TIKI TIA* WANTED THEM OFF THE FORBIDDEN GROUNDS AT ONCE. AS THE GOD HIMSELF APPEARED IN A GREAT CLOUD OF SMOKE, SCOOBY-DOO VANISHED!

FREDDIE, VELMA, AND DAPHNE PITCHED IN TO FIND SCOOBY-- AND BRAVED THE HAUNTED VILLAGE TO REVEAL MANO TIKI TIA AS NOTHING MORE THAN A HUGE *PARADE FLOAT!* THE HAWAIIAN WITCH DOCTOR WAS NONE OTHER THAN THEIR HOST, JOHN SIMMS, WHO SOUGHT TO FRIGHTEN OFF THE LOCAL FISHERMEN SO THAT HE COULD POACH THEIR *PEARLS!*

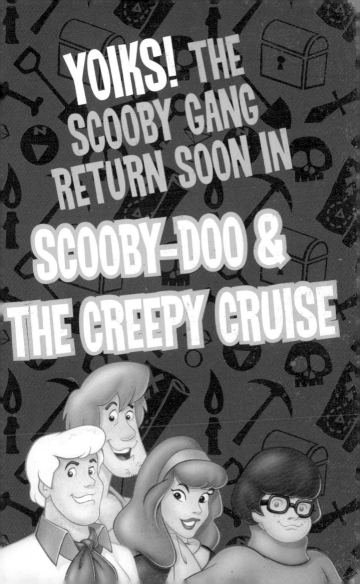